MARY INNIS ANSELL

TALES TOLD BY
THE RED-GOLD DRAGON

Dedicated to friends and relatives near and far

ISBN: 978-1-7773834-5-9 (paperback version)
ISBN: 978-1-7773834-4-2 (electronic version)
Published in Canada with cover design by Mary Ansell

CONTENTS

SIR ARTHUR'S FIRST QUEST

SIR Arthur was a young knight, named by his parents after the famous King Arthur of the Round Table. Arthur's father was only a gentleman farmer, but by careful economizing he had managed to obtain a knighthood for his son. He also gave his son a dapple-grey mare that Sir Arthur optimistically named Lightning. Although Lightning was not the liveliest horse, she was steady-going and knew her own mind.

It was the custom for young knights to go on quests to seek their fortune. On his twenty-first birthday, with a few provisions and the blessings of his parents, Sir Arthur said good-bye to them and to his little sister Genevieve and set out with Lightning on his first quest.

They had been following the road, which ran fairly straight, for about a week, when they found themselves deep inside a dense forest, confronted by a fork in the road. As they were in an unknown place, Sir Arthur followed the tradition of allowing his horse to choose which way to go. Lightning sniffed the air and promptly chose the path that led toward the tallest trees. Half an hour later, they reached a huge old oak tree, with a door in its trunk.

"This must be the very centre of the woods," thought Sir Arthur, "where the Guardian of the Forest lives." He signalled Lightning to stop, then dismounted and knocked on the door.

It was opened by a red-gold dragon with beautifully folded wings. He was only three feet long and was very old, but his eyes gleamed brightly. He looked curiously at the knight and his horse. "Good day. Is there something I can do for you?"

"Indeed, yes. I am Sir Arthur, at your service, and this is my horse Lightning. We are on our first quest but have not yet decided what to search for. Perhaps you could tell me where you have hidden your treasure hoard?"

"I am sorry, but I have no treasure," replied the dragon. "I never bothered to collect any. When I was very young, I was the pet dragon of one of the most powerful emperors of a distant land. His men found me just as I was hatching out of the egg. I was fed with delicious fruits and lay across the Emperor's feet on special occasions, when he was sitting on his throne. He would even let me sleep on the end of his bed," added the dragon, his eyes misting over at the recollection. "When the Emperor died, over one thousand years ago, I travelled the world until I found this forest and have been living here ever since. All my smoke and fire are gone now – I never had much – but I fly out from time to time and catch gnats. It keeps me going."

The Red-Gold Dragon stretched out his wings contentedly in the patch of sunlight that fell just in front of the oak tree door. He sunned himself sleepily for a few moments and then turned to look at Sir Arthur. "Why not go and see what remains of that great empire and its golden palace, with the marble courtyards, ornamental trees, and pools of many kinds of fish? It lies far to the south, in the land where the sun always shines."

"With all my heart," cried Sir Arthur, giving the dragon's paw a hearty shake. "Thank you very much for your advice. I shall most certainly follow it." He leapt onto Lightning, who had been waiting patiently, and they trotted off southward.

The dragon looked after them, smiled and shook his head and then went back to sunning himself.

Sir Arthur and Lightning jogged on for many months. At first the knight tried to guide their course by the position of the sun, but there were few roads leading directly southward, and their progress was continually being hindered by rivers, lakes, hills, and cities which got in the way. Whenever this happened, Sir Arthur would let Lightning choose their route, which she did with unerring certainty. Gradually, as they came nearer the sun, the climate became hotter and the land more arid. The leaves of the trees were smaller and a darker green, and the lizards on the sand reminded Sir Arthur of the Red-Gold Dragon.

However, after a while, the sun seemed to shine more gently, the air was cooler, and the leaves were a softer colour. Sometimes a misty rain would fall, and rabbits scampered about in the underbrush, eating pink and white clover. Sir Arthur's heart rejoiced at the sight, for it reminded him of home. Lightning, too, seemed happier and moved at a faster pace.

Then one evening, just at dusk, Lightning crested the brow of a hill. What was the knight's surprise, when he saw below him his own father's farm, with the cows just going in for milking!

He thought, "All those times, when I let Lightning choose the way, she must have slyly brought us around in a great circle."

The sight of the farm was so lovely that Sir Arthur decided then and there that what he really wanted to do was to stay at home and work the land. He only feared his parents' disappointment when they learned that he had not found anything of value to bring back with him from his quest.

However, then Lightning whinnied and galloped forward, dispelling Arthur's doubts, and his parents and Genevieve ran to greet him. When he told them of his wish to be a farmer, instead of being unhappy, his parents confessed that it was what they had been hoping for ever since he started out. Thus, Lightning and Sir Arthur were home to stay. It was the knight's twenty-second birthday.

THE BLUE JAY'S THREE WISHES

MEETING Sir Arthur and hearing him speak of his first quest reminded the Red-Gold Dragon of one of his favourite pastimes, the writing of fairy tales. Many of the tales were inspired by his experiences in that empire of long ago and other lands. He brought his fairy tale book out into the sunshine, to read the stories he had already written. This is the first tale:

Once upon a time there was a blue jay, who lived in the woods near the ocean. All day he flew from tree to tree, searching for food and screaming and calling to his friends.

One day he met a squirrel who was spreading a rumour.

"There is a creature in these woods who can grant wishes," chattered the squirrel. "This morning I wished I could find a beech nut. Would you believe it? The next moment, I saw one right in front of me! When I had eaten it, I tried again. I wished for an acorn. Almost before I had finished wishing, there it was!"

"This must be investigated!" screamed the blue jay.

He began to question all the animals who lived in the woods. Finally, he found a nuthatch who said, "The old crow who roosts in the tall pine tree near the water has the power to do anything. She can grant wishes whenever she likes!"

That very afternoon, the blue jay paid a visit to the crow and asked if it was really possible for her to grant wishes.

The crow fluffed up her feathers and looked very wise. "Of course, it is possible. And since you have taken the trouble to find me, you may have three wishes!"

The blue jay was doubtful and decided to test the crow's power by making a very difficult wish. "I wish the sky would fall!" he told the crow.

"Nothing could be simpler," she replied. "Your wish will soon come true."

At first nothing happened. However, soon it began to grow more and more misty, until a thick fog had settled over the woods.

"Fog is a type of cloud, and a cloud is part of the sky," reasoned the blue jay. "This probably happened because of my wish."

He was wondering what his second wish should be, when he overheard a conversation between two moths. One was saying to the other, "Did you see? There was a dazzling shower of falling stars last night, before the moon rose."

The jay found the crow again. "Blue jays are always awake all day," he explained, "but as soon as the sun goes down, we fall asleep. What I wish is that tonight I will stay wide awake and be able to see the moon and stars."

That evening, instead of climbing into the middle of a bush and fluffing out his feathers as he always did to keep safe and warm while sleeping, the blue jay flew to the top of a pine tree, where he would have a good view. As it grew darker and darker, he heard the hoot of an owl and saw a pair of bats swooping after insects. He was quite excited and did not feel at all sleepy.

Finally, looking upward, he could see the stars – hundreds of tiny pieces of brightness scattered over the sky. He saw a sudden streak of light and guessed it must be a shooting star. As he watched the moon climb high in the sky, he thought carefully about what his last wish should be.

On the following day, he said to the crow, "Next nesting season is the first time I'll be old enough to have a nest of my own. What I wish for is to find a perfect mate."

"You will meet her soon," promised the crow.

The blue jay was very pleased. He flew through the woods, from one clump of trees to the next, looking for other jays. Whenever he met a flock of jays, he told them about his wish and that he would soon be meeting a perfect mate.

In the third flock was a young lady jay, who, as soon as she heard the blue jay's story, was sure that she was the one the magic intended as his mate.

She hopped gracefully onto the branch where he was sitting. "I think the magic has brought you to the right place," she said. "I think I am the one you are looking for."

The blue jay had never before seen such a lovely lady jay. He found some delicious red berries and presented them to her as a courtship present.

A few days later, the other jays, the squirrel, the nuthatch and the crow all came to the wedding, which was held in the crow's pine tree near the ocean. The blue jay asked the crow to grant one more wish, a wish for a successful nesting season.

"Three wishes are enough," she said, "but I will give you some advice instead. Make sure your nest is well hidden, feed the young birds as much as possible, and don't let them explore on their own until they can fly well."

The pair followed her advice and by the end of the season had raised a brood of charming young blue jays.

SEEKING THE SEA

ONE day the Emperor painted several pictures and asked the Red-Gold Dragon to tell a story for which the pictures could serve as illustrations. This is the tale told by the dragon:

Once upon a time, there was a small bird who lived in a forest with his parents and his brothers and sisters. He was a greenish colour, but he knew that when he grew up, he would be red with black wings, like his father. He loved to eat insects and juicy green grubs. He had just reached the age of perfecting his flying and was very eager to explore the world and unravel its mysteries.

One day he met a strange orange beetle with black spots. "Who are you?" he asked. "Are you good to eat?"

She waved her antennae at him "I am a ladybug, and I am not at all good to eat."

A few days later he described to his parents how he had met a large furry animal with bright green, watching eyes, who crept along very slowly on four feet. "I let him almost reach me, to see what he would do, and then just as I was flying away up into a tree, he pounced at me. Then he scratched at the tree trunk and looked up at me, lashing his tail."

"That was a cat," explained his father. "They sometimes come into these woods, but you mustn't play with them, because they are very dangerous."

The bird's mother was anxious about him, fearing that his curiosity would be his downfall, but his father assured her that it was a necessary part of growing up and was only a phase he was going through.

It was on the morning after an extremely wet and windy night that the little bird was attracted by the sound of scolding. On arriving at the scene, he found two chipmunks pelting a very bedraggled bird with nuts and bark.

"Leave that bird alone," he cried. "He's a friend of mine." Then he asked the bird who he was, and where he came from.

"I am a tern," said the bird, "and the windstorm has blown me far out of my way. It isn't that I mind storms, it's just that I don't like to be so far from the sea."

"What is the sea?" asked the little bird.

"Have you never seen the sea? How unfortunate you are! The sea is a vast body of water, so wide that it takes days to fly across it. There are wind currents over the sea that you can find nowhere else. And then there are the animals of the sea. Far to the south there lives a bird that cannot fly but can swim under the water, using its wings as flippers. It likes to lie on its stomach in the snow and push itself down hills with its feet and wings. In other places there are sea otters that love to frolic and play in the waves, and great tortoises that live on little islands and eat thorny plants called cacti. My wings are dry now, and I can wait no longer. I am off to the sea!"

With these words, the tern flew up over the trees and away to the east. The little bird was much impressed by such boldness and immediately determined that he, too, would see the marvels of the sea. First, he went to say good-bye to his parents and to boast about his intentions to his brothers and sisters. They were rather inclined to laugh at him, but his mother, seeing that his mind was made up, gave him her blessing, warning him never to sleep on the ground and never to talk to strangers. His father was proud to have his son show so much initiative.

The little bird set off toward the rising sun, as he had seen the tern do, and flew over the forest until he was tired. By this time, it was late afternoon, and he perched in a tree to rest and to eat a few insects. When he had done this, he noticed that the tree was right at the edge of a body of water. However, since he could see across it, and there were no strange animals frolicking or eating cacti, he decided that it could not be the sea. He was startled by a loud slurping noise beneath him and looked down to see a very peculiar-looking animal having a drink. It was the largest animal he had ever seen, brownish in colour, with a long neck and a huge hump on its back. The bird was so surprised that he forgot his mother's advice about not speaking to strangers and called out, "Who are you?"

The animal finished drinking and then looked up and replied, "I am a camel. I live in a desert, which is very hot and dry, but I like to explore other parts of the world too. My friends call me 'The Wanderer'. Who are you?"

"I am a scarlet tanager, and when I grow up, I will be red with black wings. I like to explore too. I was on my way to the sea, but I got tired, so I am resting."

"I am also going that way," said the camel. "Why don't you come with me?

You can ride on my back, and then you won't feel so tired."

The bird agreed. The camel swayed from side to side as she walked, which made the bird feel a little dizzy at first, but he soon got used to it, and he and the camel became good friends.

First they crossed the water, which the camel said was a river, by finding a shallow place. The camel said that many animals could swim, but that she didn't like to very much, and that some animals such as fish could live entirely underwater. As they crossed the river, they could see the darting shapes of small fish swimming away. The camel explained that following the flow of such a large river would eventually lead them to the sea. On the other side of the river was a grassy plain, where the camel found walking easier than in the woods. The bird preferred the trees, but he didn't complain, since it was the camel who was doing the walking.

They travelled downstream, within sight of the river, for what seemed to the bird like a very long time. At night he slept on the camel's back, or in one of the few trees scattered here and there on the plain. In the daytime, the bird sometimes flew high up into the air to see what was ahead of them and then flew down again and told the camel what he had seen. The camel thought it must be wonderful to be able to fly, but the bird was so used to it by now that it seemed very natural to him. As the camel walked along with the little bird riding on her back, they observed the wildlife of the plains – snakes slithering away through the grass, strange rodents and insects, and vultures wheeling high in the sky. The camel told the bird all about life in the desert, and in return the bird described what it was like to live in the forest. The camel, who was kind-hearted, soon noticed that the more the bird talked about his parents and brothers and sisters and the juicy grubs of the forest, the more he sighed, and the sadder he grew. It was clear that the little bird was homesick.

The camel asked the bird what he knew about the sea and heard about the animals the bird expected to find there. That night, while her friend was sleeping in a tree, the camel secretly went ahead to a large lake that was in their path and persuaded the otters and turtles there to put on a convincing performance when he and the bird would 'discover' the lake the next day.

The mist was still on the lake when they arrived early the next morning, and it was impossible to see across to the other side. The otters frolicked so entertainingly, and the turtles told such tales of the prickliness of the cacti they had to eat that the little bird was quite convinced and was eager to go home and boast that he had seen the sea.

This he joyfully did, accompanied by the camel, who accepted his invitation to visit the forest. The bird's family was very glad to welcome him back, and he proudly showed his friend the camel all the sights of the forest. Best of all, when the little bird discovered that his brothers had changed their plumage during his absence, he peered over his shoulder at his own back and wings and found that he too had grown up and become a red bird with black wings!

THE SHY STORY

ONCE upon a time there was a story that was so shy it did not want to be told. It was one of the stories of the Red-Gold Dragon, who lived in an oak tree in the heart of the forest. The story asked the Red-Gold Dragon not to tell it.

"But why don't you want to be told? Usually that is what stories like most."

"I don't see how they could," said the story. "I don't like it at all. Don't you remember the first time you told me? You told me to the big cart horse who took a rest here, and he fell asleep!"

"You shouldn't feel badly about that," said the Red-Gold Dragon. "You know I found out afterward that he only likes stories which mention oats and apples."

"And then you told me to two tree swallows," continued the story. "At first, they wouldn't stay still to listen, and then they laughed at me. And then you told me to a wandering prince, and he said he didn't understand me. Every time you tell me I feel worse. Please, don't tell me again."

"You really shouldn't be upset," said the dragon. "The tree swallows are only light-hearted, and the prince takes everything too seriously. I'm sure they didn't mean to hurt your feelings."

"All the same, I'd much rather you didn't tell me again. Who knows what might happen the next time?"

The dragon thought for a while and then said, "What we need to do is to find you the right kind of audience. Once you have had the feeling of being appreciated, then I think you will probably get over feeling shy, and you will like being told. That's the way it is with most stories. It doesn't make them feel badly if the audience falls asleep or laughs. They always like to be heard."

The story was very doubtful about this, but the Red-Gold Dragon suggested, "I know what would be the best audience for you – a cat. You will know whether the cat appreciates you, because if she is pleased, she will purr. And I am sure she will purr, because, after all, you are a good story."

The story felt a little better at hearing the dragon's praise.

"There is a cat who lives only half an hour from here, who always likes to hear a story," continued the dragon. "It's a warm day – she's probably sunning herself now. Let's go and find her."

The story couldn't help feeling a little excited to think that perhaps there was someone who might like to hear it. It agreed to go with the dragon, and they flew through the trees for half an hour, until they came to the part of the forest where the cat lived. They found her sunning herself on a branch, and they landed in a tree nearby, within easy speaking distance.

"It's a fine day, isn't it?" said the dragon. "I thought you might like to hear a story you haven't heard before."

"Certainly," said the cat. "How kind of you to think of it!"

"I'm rather shy," said the story, "so, please, don't laugh or fall asleep if you can help it."

"The Red-Gold Dragon is such a good story-teller," said the cat, "and chooses his stories so well, that I shall be very surprised if I can keep myself from purring."

The Red-Gold Dragon began telling

the story, and the cat stretched herself out on the branch and closed her eyes. It looked as though she might be falling asleep, but after a few moments she began to purr. Then she purred a little louder and purred just quietly enough that she could still hear the story.

When the story was finished, the cat sat up and opened her eyes. "What a wonderful story!" she exclaimed. "I'm very pleased you came to tell it to me."

The story was delighted. "Do you still feel shy?" asked the dragon.

"I'm still a little shy," replied the story, "but the cat is a perfect audience. If you tell me again, to someone else, could the cat be there too?"

"I wouldn't mind that," said the cat. "You're the kind of story one doesn't get tired of. I'll be pleased to hear you as many times as the Red-Gold Dragon wants to tell you."

The Red-Gold Dragon and the story flew home, and the next several times the Red-Gold Dragon told the story, they made sure the cat was part of the audience. Every time the story heard the cat purring while it was being told, it felt more and more confident, until finally it was not afraid of any audience, whether the cat was there or not. Even if there was an audience where someone fell asleep, and someone else laughed or said the story was too difficult to understand, the story didn't mind, because in its imagination it could still hear the purring of the cat.

THE THREE SISTERS

THIS is the story belonging to the Red-Gold Dragon that was too shy to be told, until it was reassured by the purring of the cat:

Once upon a time there were three sisters. When the eldest was twenty-one, their fairy godmother appeared to them and said, "As you know, I have three wishes to divide among you. The time has come for each of you to make your wish."

The first sister, although she was quite good-looking, was concerned about her freckles, the shape of her nose, and other imperfections in her appearance. She wished to be beautiful, and immediately her complexion cleared, her nose assumed an elegant shape, and she was as beautiful as the day.

The second sister, who loved to read books about knightly valour and was ashamed because she was afraid to grasp a stinging nettle, wished to be brave, which she instantly became.

The third sister, who had a rather hasty temper and sometimes said things which she afterward regretted, wished to be kind. And from that time on, she was never angry and was never anything but kind.

It was not long after this that a sea monster anchored himself at the mouth of the harbour and swore that he would devour every ship that passed unless the townsfolk fed him a maiden a day.

On the first day, the beautiful sister volunteered herself, for she was also vain and was sure that the sea monster would succumb to her charms and be willing to do her behests. However, when she went out to the end of the rocky point at the mouth of the harbour and called sweetly to the monster, it came greedily toward her and took her in its jaws, for monsters have different ideas of beauty than people do. However, when it tasted the face cream which she had lavishly smeared on, it wrinkled up its nose in disgust and spat her out. She returned home safely, but the thought of the monster's ignominious treatment of her stamped a perpetual scowl on her face, which made her look quite ugly.

On the second day, the brave sister volunteered, for she was also foolhardy and didn't care whether the sea monster ate her or not. However, she had taken to wearing a hair shirt and holding a nettle in each hand to show her courage, and when the monster took her in its jaws, it spat her out because she was so prickly. After her friends had recovered from their relief at her escape, they began to tease her about being so unpalatable to the monster. Although she was invincible in the face of physical danger, she was very touchy when it came to verbal jeers and soon became a veritable coward, afraid to go into the town for fear someone might see her and make fun of her.

On the third day, the kind sister volunteered herself, for she could not bear to think of anyone else suffering when she might do instead. She also felt sorry for the sea monster, who, because of the inedibility of her sisters, had had nothing to eat for two days. With the help of the local fishermen, she discovered the types of fish and seaweed that the monster liked best and prepared a delectable brew for him.

When she offered him the food, he said that it was the first time anyone had ever been kind to him. After he had eaten his meal, the sea monster told her that because of her kindness, he would not eat her, and that she had saved the town. Then he swam off to haunt the next town up the coast.

The town did great honour to the kind sister for getting rid of the monster. She tried to share the credit with her older sisters, since they had volunteered themselves first, but in spite of all she could do, her eldest sister was unanimously considered ugly and her second sister cowardly. However, not only was the kind sister acknowledged to be kind, but there were some people who thought her brave and others who thought her beautiful.

The moral of the story is: Be kind,
and fate will be kind to you.

THE TURQUOISE LAKE

IN a valley surrounded by mountains was a turquoise lake. Pine-clad slopes rose steeply from the lakeshore on all sides but the south, where there was a broad plain. The lake remained undisturbed for many centuries, until a king, seeking a place to set up his court, sent out scouts who discovered it. They were delighted with the spot and made a glowing report to the king, persuading him that the location would be easy to defend, and that the plain would be perfect for farming. The king was convinced. Soon a magnificent palace was built, and each of the peasants who had accompanied the king to this new location was given a piece of land to farm.

The soil was fertile, and the kingdom prospered. However, for some reason the king conceived a fear of the lake itself. He decreed that no one should go near its shores for any reason and set two guards to watch over his young son, the prince, to prevent him from even seeing the lake, if possible. To make up for this, the king gave his son a small poodle that was as white as the snow. The prince named his pet Star, and she became his constant companion.

Naturally, the prince was very curious about the lake which was thought to be so dangerous. Thus, on the king's birthday, when everyone was busy preparing for the feast, he seized the opportunity to explore. Holding Star tightly in his arms, the prince slipped unnoticed out of the palace, out of the village, and down to the very shore of the turquoise lake. He might not have gone further, but Star wriggled out of his grasp and began to do some exploring of her own. Before the prince's astonished eyes, Star ran out onto the lake – on top of the waves! The prince caught her in his arms again when she returned to the land. Clutching her firmly, he gingerly tested the water with one foot, to see if it would bear his weight. The surface seemed quite strong, and he set off across the lake. Under his feet, small waves rose and fell.

He had almost reached the middle of the lake when, without warning, he felt as if he and Star were being pulled downward by a turquoise whirlpool. In a few moments, they found themselves in a courtyard paved with shadowy green marble tiles. In one corner was a swirling mass of playful poodles with long green hair, like seaweed. When they saw Star, they scrambled across the courtyard, pushing, shoving, and yapping. They began to describe to Star their games of leapfrog and chasing fish. Then, exchanging sly looks, they started to tell of the times when they had ridden seahorses, milked sea cows and teased sea serpents and giant clams. Star, who was very excited, tried to escape from the prince's arms to join the other poodles, but the prince, not quite liking the situation, fled with her down a dark hallway which opened off the courtyard.

On either side of him were doorways, but he paid no attention to them until he came to one with what looked like seaweed floating out of it. When he peered cautiously into the room, he discovered that the seaweed was actually the hair of a woman who was pulling strands of water from a basin beside her and spinning them into thread so fine that the eye could scarcely see it. In another part of the room, women were weaving the thread to make a transparent material. Star barked, and the women looked up, startled.

The prince bowed politely. "Star and I were taking a walk and accidentally fell down your whirlpool. Would you please show us the way out?"

The women who were weaving looked aghast at this proposal, but the one who was spinning said, "This boy is a prince, and therefore his word is his bond. If he will promise not to tell anyone what he has seen, I shall blindfold him and lead him and Star up the back staircase."

The prince, who was by now eager to return with Star to the safety of the palace, readily promised to keep his adventure a secret. As she led him toward the staircase, the woman explained that her people had lived there in peace for eons, but with the coming of the king and his court, they were doing what they had long neglected to do. To protect themselves, they were weaving an impenetrable surface for the lake. They had finished all but the very centre of the lake, where a whirlpool still remained. As she ceased speaking, the woman removed the prince's blindfold and gave him a gentle push.

He found himself in the back kitchen, where the master cook was putting the finishing touches on an immense birthday cake for the king. Everyone was much too intent on the cake to notice the prince, and he escaped to his room without having been missed. His two guards were testing the contents of a royal wine jar to see whether it was fit for the king's table.

For several days, the prince kept a close watch on Star, afraid that she would try to return to the lake to play with the mischievous seaweed poodles. These fears proved justified, for one day when he was called to the court tailor to try on a new suit of clothes, he returned to find that Star had vanished. His guards had been very lax of late, and the prince was able to elude them and run down to the lakeshore. He didn't stop until he had reached the middle of the lake. However, he saw that the lake people had finished their work. The impenetrable surface of the lake was complete, and the whirlpool was gone.

Then the prince remembered that Star had not been blindfolded on the way up the secret staircase. He retraced his steps to the back kitchen, which was deserted at that time of day. However, there were no stairs to be seen. He was at a loss until the huge old grandfather clock by the fireplace suddenly struck two. On the first stroke, the door of the clock opened, revealing a dark, dank stairway. On the second stroke the prince darted through the doorway, just before it closed.

The stairs were lit by a dim turquoise glow, which grew brighter as he descended toward the lake. After what seemed like hundreds of stairs, he reached the bottom, where he saw a long hallway before him. In the distance, he heard the poodles yapping, He ran toward the sound as fast as he could, calling Star's name as he went. Finally, the hallway made a sudden turn, and there was the courtyard where he had been before. Star was crouched in a corner, and all the other poodles were prancing around her, pretending to nip her ears and teasing her because her hair was not long and turquoise, like theirs. When she saw the prince, Star gave a joyful yelp, broke through the ranks of poodles and leapt into his arms. He turned and sped away. The poodles followed them halfway down the hall before turning back, but the prince continued to run until he arrived, out of breath, at the top of the staircase. He gave the door a push and tumbled into the dark kitchen. It was only half past two, but the grandfather clock struck three, and the door would never open again after that.

The prince and Star never told anyone about their adventures, and the people of the turquoise lake continue to live in peace in their secret realm.

THE STICKLEBACK FISH

ONCE upon a time, in a slow-moving river in a flat, grassy country, lived a fish. He was called a stickleback fish, because of the spines on his back. The sun shone almost every day, and all the fish that lived in the river had everything they needed to eat. Each day the stickleback hunted for food and then swam slowly up and down the river. On the river bottom there were weeds, sandy patches, and sand-coloured stones, while on the riverbank there were green reeds, grass, and a few bushes. The stickleback often thought he would like to see something else – but what? Perhaps there was nothing else to see.

One day he met an eel who was swimming upstream.

"Please excuse me," said the stickleback politely, "may I ask you something?"

The eel stopped swimming and said, "Well?"

"I know you travel long distances. Is everywhere the same as here? Or is there anywhere I could see something different?"

"Every place is different from every other place, of course," said the eel. But I know something you might like to see. There is a wonderful catalpa tree in bloom on the bank of the next river. It is supposed to be enchanted."

The stickleback thanked the eel and at once decided to visit the catalpa tree. Before setting out, he told a much older stickleback his plans.

The older fish said, "After your travels, you will probably want to return here. My advice is to make sure to bring back something with you, so that you will have some lasting benefit from your experience."

"I'll do what I can," promised the stickleback, growing excited at the thought of his journey.

He began to swim downstream. He swam and swam all day, but the scenery didn't change. However, on the second day, he noticed some kinds of river plants he had never seen before, and on the third day, he reached the open water of a broad lake. The sun glinted on the rippling surface, and great white spoonbills and black-and-white avocets waded near the shore. The stickleback followed a reed bank around the end of the lake, until he felt a slight current caused by another river. Swimming against the flow of water, he crossed a wide belt of reeds and then found himself swimming between riverbanks lined with trees. He continued upstream, searching both sides of the river for a tree in bloom. Finally, he caught sight of a school of brilliantly coloured orange fish who were doing loops and turns under a huge tree covered with white blossoms.

A gentle breeze shook the hundreds of flowers, the sweet smell of nectar permeated the air, and the hum of bees seemed to cast a drowsy spell over all nearby. The stickleback gazed at the splendour above him, feeling as if he were at the edge of a magical world.

All at once he was surrounded by the school of brilliantly coloured fish.

"It's a stickleback fish!" they cried. "There hasn't been a stickleback here for years. You've come to admire the catalpa tree, haven't you?"

"Yes, of course. It makes me feel very happy just to look at it. I wish there was something so lovely in my own river. Everything there is only green or brown. What a wonderful colour you all are! Have you been enchanted by swimming under the catalpa tree?"

All the fish laughed. "Of course not. We are goldfish, and this is our natural colour."

The stickleback, remembering his conversation with the older fish, decided to ask the goldfish if they knew of anything he might be able to take back to his own river.

"You should wait here until the Red-Gold Dragon arrives. He's sure to be able to help you. Have you seen him yet? He's been coming here every day since the catalpa tree started blooming. He loves the smell of the flowers."

The stickleback had no intention of leaving as long as the catalpa tree was in bloom. He swam with the golden carp, admired the dragonflies with blue wings that hovered over the water, and stopped every few minutes to look with delight at the catalpa tree. Then he saw a dragon approaching that was about the size of a large eagle.

''Here he is!'' cried the goldfish.

The Red-Gold Dragon glided low over the water, swooped up under the heart-shaped leaves of the catalpa tree and landed on a low branch overhanging the river.

After waiting until the dragon had had time to enjoy the smell of the flowers, the stickleback introduced himself and asked for advice.

"I wish I could bring something back with me that would make my river as attractive as this one. I wish I could bring back the catalpa tree itself, the goldfish and some of the blue-winged dragonflies."

The dragon liked this idea. "I know what we could do, although it would take a long time. If you like, I can take some of last year's seed pods from this tree and plant the seeds along the banks of your river. Then in a few years, catalpa trees will be growing there."

"How marvellous!" cried the stickleback. "Perhaps the second part of my wish could come true too. Would any of you goldfish be willing to live in my river? There is plenty of food for every type of fish."

"We'll all come!" they cried. "There are many schools of goldfish living in this river – they won't miss us. And we can come back here every year, when the catalpa tree is in bloom, until your trees grow up."

The stickleback was so happy, he leapt into the air. "Maybe some of these dragonflies will come too. What is the use of the sun shining day after day, if there are no beautiful things for it to shine on?"

The stickleback and the goldfish enjoyed themselves under the catalpa tree, and the Red-Gold Dragon came for a visit every day, until the tree had finished blooming, and the last flower petals had fallen from the tree into the river. Then the Red-Gold Dragon collected a few seed pods and flew overland to plant the seeds, while the stickleback led the school of goldfish and some of the dragonflies, who had decided to come, back to his own river.

When the stickleback introduced his new friends to the fish in his home river, the goldfish recognised the older stickleback as the one who had visited their river years before. He was overjoyed at the use the young stickleback had made of his advice.

Every year the stickleback and the goldfish travelled to see the catalpa tree in bloom, until one year the trees that had grown from the seeds planted by the dragon had so many blossoms that the fish decided not to leave their own river. From that time on, the Red-Gold Dragon visited every year, and the river became so famous that fish from faraway rivers came to swim under the catalpa trees.

THE WATER EMERALD

ONCE upon a time, there was a river nymph who lived in the water with the rest of her kin near the source of a great river, high up in the mountains. She loved beautiful things and had made herself what she called a 'water emerald' by weaving spells about a patch of water shadowed by overhanging deep green grass. The emerald was sharp-edged and as clear as glass and was also magical, for it could think and feel. She was very pleased with it and set it into the gold brooch that fastened her sea-green cloak.

The time came for her to make the pilgrimage made once in the life of every nymph – a journey through each of the Seven Seas, in order to learn about the ways of the world. She said good-bye to her home and to the other nymphs, fastened her brooch more securely and let the water carry her downstream.

For a while, the familiar mountains still loomed overhead, and the rush of the water was fast and steep, but presently the land levelled and the river became a broad lake. The river nymph had never before seen so much water collected in one place. She was swimming leisurely through the lake, watching the fish and listening to what the water was saying, when suddenly she saw a great, green scaly water monster. With a flip of his tail, he tried to catch her, but she darted away, down into the river which flowed out of the lake. The monster was almost upon her, so she snatched the jewel from her brooch and threw it into the water to distract him. The emerald glinted brightly and caught the monster's eye, while the nymph instantly disappeared from view. The enraged monster lunged after her, but she was gone. When he came back to vent his wrath on the green stone, the friendly river had covered it with silt, and he could not find it. Disgusted, he swam away to other waters.

The nymph was forced to leave her jewel where it was, since one of the conditions of her pilgrimage was that she must not turn back until she had swum each of the Seven Seas. However, the emerald was perfectly content to remain there, for it knew that she would eventually return.

As soon as the monster had gone, the river uncovered the emerald, so that it could see and enjoy its surroundings. For many days it watched the pale blue water flowing by, and the graceful green water weeds, insect larvae and fish. Every so often, the emerald was tumbled farther downstream by the force of the river, until it was near a large city.

A fisherman, on his way to his morning's catch, thought he saw a green glow in the water. When he rowed his boat over to the spot, he saw that it was caused by light reflected from a jewel resting on the bottom of the river. He fished it out with a net, and it dimmed a little on leaving the water.

Now that the gemstone was in his hand, the fisherman considered what profit he could make from his good fortune. He had a small daughter, and his one ambition was to bring her up properly. After turning things over in his mind, he decided not to keep the jewel, nor give it to his daughter, but to make a present of it to the greatest lord of the city and then see what happened.

Accordingly, the lord received the fisherman's gift, which pleased him so much that he engaged the fisherman to be the sole supplier of fish for his lordship's table. The fisherman was well satisfied with this arrangement since it guaranteed him a steady income.

The lord had a gold ring made to provide a setting for his jewel and wore it constantly. He loved to look into the emerald's pure green depths and amused himself by fancying he saw visions there. Once he imagined he saw a green-cloaked nymph swimming in a far-off sea, but most of the time it seemed as if he saw rivers, and rushing water, and green grass over the water. However, then he noticed that the stone was losing colour, growing paler day by day and more watery-looking. He thought it cruel that such a lovely thing should fade, and the idea troubled him. He began unaccountably to haunt the riverbanks and astonished his fun-loving friends by becoming quiet and reserved.

The lord's house had a balcony overhanging the river, and he went to sit there one evening, feeling very sad. His hand wearing the ring rested on the rail of the balcony, and the jewel was almost the colour of rain. Suddenly he felt a splash of river water on his hand, and the emerald glinted brilliantly green for an instant. He heard the faintest swirl in the water and, looking down, saw the river nymph with her green cloak and long hair floating in the water. She had swum each of the Seven Seas and had seen many interesting and wonderful things. Now she was on her way home.

"Who are you, and what do you want?" asked the lord.

"I am a river nymph, and I have come for my water emerald. You may as well give it back to me, because if you don't, it will die, and that would be a pity. I will give you a real emerald in exchange, that I found in the Green Sea."

She threw him the real emerald, which he caught, while the water emerald appeared to melt out of the clasp that held it and fell into the river nymph's waiting hands. She returned it to her brooch, where it immediately regained its original brilliance. Then she and the jewel, now shining brightly, disappeared homeward up the river.

The lord found that his new emerald fitted his ring perfectly and took great pleasure in showing it to the members of his court. He soon regained his customary good spirits, and the fish supplied by the fisherman were always excellent.

THE SMALLEST CROW

ONCE upon a time, a crow family lived in a forest near the ocean. As the young crows grew up, they were all very happy except for the youngest, who was much smaller than the others. The smallest crow could not do what he wanted, because the other crows often pecked him. Whenever there was something to eat, he had to wait until the others were finished before he could have anything.

One day, feeling both unhappy and hungry, he decided to leave his family and look for food on his own. There were many crows, and the whole forest was divided into territories, each occupied by a crow family. Thus, the smallest crow knew he could not look for anything to eat in the forest; he must go to the ocean shore.

Along the shore were rocks, mussels, snails, and seagulls. The crow watched seagulls take mussels in their beaks, fly up high in the air and then drop the mussels onto the rocks below to break their shells, in order to eat the mussels. However, the crow soon found a better method. He learned how to grip a mussel tightly with his claws so that he could use his strong pointed beak to pry open the shell and eat the tasty meat inside. It was possible to reach the mussels only at low tide, because at high tide they were deep under the water. Therefore, the crow carefully studied the times of the tides. He also discovered how to pick up small rocks to catch the little animals hiding beneath. Once he had got used to life on the ocean shore, the smallest crow was able to eat his fill every day and felt content, although there were times when he was a little lonely.

The following year, in the summer, there was almost no rain. The crow heard that the forest was very dry, that food was scarce and that the birds living in the forest were not in good health. He considered the situation. Along the ocean shore, mussels were plentiful – perhaps he could help the crows in the forest. For the first time, he returned home to visit his family.

All of them were hungry, and the smallest crow invited them to come with him to the shore. Seeing how healthy he looked, they immediately agreed. The other crows in the forest were also hungry and decided to follow him as well.

The smallest crow led the way to the ocean shore. He taught the other crows how to pry open mussel shells, how to hunt the small animals living under the rocks and how to avoid the waves. At the same time, he calculated the time of the tide and told the other crows when the next low tide would be.

Seeing this, the other crows realised how clever he was, and they all decided to choose him as their leader. When the drought was over, he returned to the forest with the others. After that, the other crows always made sure that the best of whatever there was to eat, and whenever there were difficulties, they looked to him for advice.

Igravaine

THERE was a tent at the bottom of the meadow, where no tent ought to be. Probably a knight's pavilion? But no knight had the right to trespass on the land of another, even if the other was mainly a farmer. Knights were a nuisance. If asked to move, they were likely to use it as an excuse to have a practice fight – and naturally Tresson wasn't carrying his lance.

"Besides, we're out of practice, aren't we?" he said, stroking his horse's neck. Tresson was sure that his horse, a beautiful bay, had no more objection than he did to herding cows instead of risking his life on the battlefield. Tresson's horse sniffed the air. "Yes, he's a beauty, isn't he?" said Tresson, looking across the field at the knight's horse grazing near the tent.

It was nearly dusk. Tresson and his horse, Beaugard, were making a last inspection of some of the back meadows before going home for the night. "We'll let the knight and his horse stay there for now," said Tresson. "With any luck they'll move on somewhere else in the morning." He turned Beaugard away and was just taking a final glance back over his shoulder, when a light appeared in the tent. "Whoa, Beaugard," he called softly.

The glow flickered unsteadily, lighting up the brown tent walls. It must be some kind of lantern. The knight was obviously arranging his belongings and was taking off his armour to go to sleep. When he stepped in front of the lantern, his shadow was plainly to be seen on the wall of the tent. But when the armour was removed, what was revealed was the shadow of a woman!

"A woman dressed in armour?" thought Tresson. "Surely there is only one person inside the tent. But is it likely that a woman would be travelling by herself, dressed as a knight? And in such a remote part of the country?"

As he watched, the light went out. "Probably it is a knight and lady travelling together," he said to Beaugard. "I suppose that horse could carry two people easily enough."

It might be a good idea to make sure. He clucked to Beaugard, and they picked their way across the meadow. The knight's horse lifted his head and stamped his hoof as they came near. "That horse is standing guard," thought Tresson.

He cleared his throat and said in a stern tone, "Sir knight! I wish to have speech with you!"

"I have already lain down to sleep. What is it you want?" replied a man's voice.

"I am honoured that you and your lady have chosen one of my meadows for a camping place," said Tresson. "However, I would advise you not to remain here, as a herd of cattle will be coming this way in the morning."

"I thank you for your courtesy," answered the knight, "but I am tired and would be grateful to remain here until the first light."

"Very well," said Tresson. However, he added to himself, "The thing to do is to come over this way at dawn tomorrow, to make sure the knight and his lady really do leave."

Tresson was ready to return home, but Beaugard seemed to want to meet the knight's horse. Beaugard walked deliberately to where the other horse was standing, and they touched noses.

"Beautiful horse," murmured Tresson, "and he's been kept in top condition. That knight clearly knows something about horses and cares about them too." He reached out and stroked the horse's nose. "But we didn't come here to make friends."

He signalled to Beaugard that he was serious about leaving this time, and they galloped over the darkened field.

The next morning, the sky was just beginning to grow light as Tresson dismounted at the edge of the woods which overlooked the back meadow. The tent was still there, and the knight's horse looked as if he were sleeping. Birds had already started to sing, and the deep blue of the sky was becoming paler moment by moment.

Tresson sat on a fallen tree trunk to wait, but before he had a chance to get comfortable, Beaugard shifted and pricked his ears forward. Tresson saw the knight's horse give himself a shake and then heard a faint sound of pieces of armour and chain mail jingling together. The knight was getting up.

In a few minutes, dressed in full armour, the knight stepped out of the tent, went to his horse and began packing the saddlebags. But where was the lady? Perhaps she was taking her time getting dressed. There was still no sign of her when the knight began slackening the tent ropes. Finally, he disappeared into the tent and then backed out, holding the lower end of the central tent pole and letting the walls of the tent collapse gradually into folds.

There had been only one person in the tent. Then the knight must be a woman in armour! Tresson watched as she folded and rolled up the tent. Something like that was hard to do while dressed in armour, but she looked as if she had done it hundreds of times. She strapped the tent behind her horse's saddle and then swung herself up, ready to leave.

Tresson mounted Beaugard and trotted toward them. The knight lowered her visor as they approached and began to ride away, however her horse turned his head toward them and whinnied, clearly remembering Beaugard from the night before.

"You have nothing to fear from us," called Tresson, "but I would like to give you some advice."

The knight's hand tightened on her lance, but her words were courteous. "Naturally I would like to profit from your advice," said the knight in a man's voice that almost made Tresson doubt what he had seen. However, he rode forward, throwing back his cloak to show that he was not armed and had no harmful intentions.

"If you want to keep your identity as a woman a secret," he said, "you should take care not to step between the lantern and the walls of your tent. Your shadow gave you away."

Startled, the knight signalled her horse to stop and stared Tresson straight in the eye for several seconds. Tresson could see only the gleam of eyes in the shadow of the visor. Then she seemed to be satisfied and suddenly relaxed.

"That is good advice," she said, still in a deep voice. "Usually I am more careful but, if you will forgive me, I had thought this part of the country was uninhabited."

Tresson laughed. "No, I have a large piece of land here, which supports myself and my herd of milk cattle."

"Since you discovered my secret accidentally, I hope you will be willing to tell no one," said the woman knight.

"Naturally I will keep it to myself. May I know your name? I am Tresson of the Larchental, and my horse is called Beaugard."

But at this, the woman knight became angry. "How can you ask my name when it is obvious that I wish to keep my identity a secret?"

Tresson did not answer but signalled Beaugard to turn, and they galloped away out of sight.

The woman knight gazed after them. "So, Gryphon," she said, stroking her horse's mane, "it seems we have insulted them."

"He was wrong to ask my name," she thought, "but perhaps I need not have answered so rudely. He could have tried to make trouble for me, but instead, he gave me good advice."

"Come, Gryphon," she said, "we have a long way to go." Like Tresson, she was in the habit of addressing remarks to her horse when no one else was nearby. As they crossed the meadow, it occurred to her that they had been Tresson's guests, since they had camped on his land the night before. "Certainly, I should have been more courteous," she thought. "I was rude because I was concerned that someone had discovered my secret."

They climbed a track through the woods and came to a small, grassy hill. On all sides there was rolling countryside of grass and trees. "This would be an easy place to get lost," she thought. "The main road must be somewhere close by, but it is completely hidden from view."

An hour later they found themselves in thick woods, no longer sure of their direction. As they passed a dense clump of trees, they startled a great stag, that bounded ahead of them and disappeared.

"That stag probably knows every inch of this forest," she said. "Let us follow him."

They soon came to a steep ravine. There was a faint trail visible where the stag had descended, but the ground was too rocky and thickly overgrown for a horse and rider to follow. As they continued along the edge of the ravine, it became wider and deeper. The sides of the valley were covered with trees, and a lovely river gleamed at the bottom of it.

"If only I were not so hungry and thirsty," thought the woman knight, as she led Gryphon through the forest, "I would think this was one of the most beautiful places I have ever seen."

The valley gradually became more open, and she paused to look down into it. She was surprised to see someone sitting on a rock near the river. Surely that was Tresson, with his horse! Tresson seemed to be idly throwing stones into the water.

"He doesn't seem particularly pleased with life, does he?" she said. "I am afraid I put him in an ill humour this morning. He was helpful toward us, and I was discourteous in return. Come,

Gryphon. We ought to go and apologise now that we have the opportunity."

Here the sides of the valley sloped more gently, and she was able to lead Gryphon down the hill.

Beaugard whinnied, and Tresson looked up and saw the approaching knight and horse. What were they doing? Perhaps they were lost! He should have stayed to make sure they were on the right path, instead of riding away. He waved to show them where they could cross the river.

Traversing a series of stepping stones, the woman knight guided her horse through the shallow water beside her.

As she reached Tresson, she pulled off her gauntlet and held out her hand. "I crave your pardon. After you left, I realised that since you had permitted us to spend the night in your meadow, we were your guests, and I had behaved very rudely."

He grasped her hand. "You did nothing wrong. It was I who lacked courtesy. I should at least have showed you the way to the main road. I know that the paths in this area are like a maze."

The woman knight laughed. "You are perfectly right. We lost our way. But I am glad to have the chance to apologise."

He wondered why she continued to speak in the deep voice of a knight but said nothing about it. "Perhaps you are hungry? If so, I have food to spare. I have brought my breakfast and lunch with me and so far, have eaten nothing."

"I will not deceive you. It is true that I am hungry, but I cannot accept food without paying for it, and at the moment I have no money."

"It is good to behave honourably," said Tresson, "but not so good to go hungry. If you are willing to do some work in exchange for a meal, there is something you could help me with."

"Gladly."

"Sometimes the river here is so deep that it flows over the stepping stones. There are two fallen trees nearby which have come down the slope. If you could help me to position one of them so that it crosses the river to serve as a bridge, I would be greatly in your debt."

The woman knight was pleased. "That is just such work as I like to do! Let us look at the logs."

She was very strong and also soon thought of a way of harnessing Beaugard and Gryphon so that they could help to move one of the logs. By leading the horses back across the river, where they could pull from the other side, it was possible to manoeuvre the larger log so that it spanned the river at a narrow point between two high rocks.

"Many thanks," said Tresson. "Without you and Gryphon, my idea of making a bridge would have remained a dream."

He quickly opened his saddlebag and brought out bread and thick hunks of meat and cheese. "Eat all you like. You will have a long way to go before finding the next inn."

"I thank you for your hospitality," said the woman knight. "To make amends for my earlier rudeness, I shall tell you my name." She took off her helmet, and her long hair fell about her shoulders. "I am Igravaine."

"Do you wear armour only as a disguise?" asked Tresson. "Or do you travel as a knight from joust to joust?"

"That has been my way of life for the past several years. I practise constantly and am fortunate in having an excellent horse. I am able to win enough in prizes to feed myself and Gryphon and to keep my armour in good condition."

"But is it not dangerous? What happens when you are wounded?"

"Then I find some other work, until I have recovered."

"If you can find other work, why do you risk your life at jousting?"

"There is no other work that I like so well. And it means that Gryphon and I can work together."

Igravaine continued to speak always in the deep voice of a knight. At last, Tresson said, "I wish that you would not disguise your voice. No one comes here but myself, and there is no need to disguise it from me, now that you have told me your name."

"I am sorry not to grant your request," said Igravaine, "but I dare not. When I first put on armour, I determined always to speak in a deep voice, even when I speak only to myself, or to Gryphon, when we are alone. In this way, the habit is so strong that I can be sure I will never give myself away in a moment of danger." She got to her feet. "We must now be on our way. I would be obliged if you would tell me how to reach the road to Beckern."

Tresson did so and then added, "If you should chance to come this way again, I hope you will do me the honour of making your presence known. If you do not despise working with cows, you could earn some supper, as well as lunch."

Igravaine smiled a real smile for the first time. "You are very kind. It happens that there is a joust at the beginning of next month in the city of Drayberg. I believe there is a shortcut in that direction which runs across your land."

"Yes, it is a good route until the snow falls and should still be passable then."

"Thank you once more for your hospitality," said Igravaine, as she set off for Beckern.

"I should guess that Sir Tresson cares little for fighting," she said to Gryphon, as they reached the main road, "but he is a courteous and well-intentioned knight. When we come this way again, we should show equal courtesy and bring him a gift of some sort."

The grand prize at Beckern consisted of money, as well as a golden medallion. If she won, she would be able to give Tresson the medallion. It had a certain value and was also a gift of honour.

At the Beckern tournament, Igravaine planned her strategy carefully. She studied the other knights as they were practising and, on the day of the joust, managed to make sure that she fought her strongest opponents while she was still fresh. Between clashes, she dismounted from Gryphon, so that he would not grow tired, and together they were able to defeat all of the knights who rode against them. Since no one else had done so well, she was declared the champion of the tournament. She received the prize and, as was her custom after a victory, immediately left the area at a gallop, to discourage anyone who might want to challenge her for the money.

In two days, she reached the Larchental and gave Tresson the medallion.

"I already know your strength from the help which you gave me in moving the log," said Tresson, "but I confess I am amazed that you have been able to vanquish so many knights. Surely not every knight you meet is weaker than yourself?"

"No, naturally most of them are stronger, but then I must ride so that they will strike either too soon, or too late."

"I hope that we shall always fight on the same side," said Tresson. "I will keep your gift as the token of a valuable ally." He persuaded Igravaine to stay for a day or two, to help him cut wood for the fires used in making cheese.

She agreed but refused to sleep indoors, preferring to camp where Gryphon could graze next to the tent. She proved to be highly skilled in wielding an axe and asked many questions, so that she could understand the workings of the farm. She enjoyed herself greatly, but on the third day the air turned colder, and she knew that she must leave at once, to go over the pass to Drayberg before the snow fell.

"Probably I will not see you this winter," she said to Tresson, "but I hope next spring or summer I will be able to come this way again."

He was reluctant to see her leave, for the more he saw of her, the more he admired her daring, intelligence, and sense of honour. He knew that the tournament in Drayberg was a large one, attended by knights from distant places and that it could be dangerous.

However, Igravaine was obviously accustomed to danger.

Therefore, he wished her well and said only, "You know you are welcome to come here whenever you feel like doing a little farming."

Drayberg was several days' ride from the pass. When Igravaine reached it, the city was already full to overflowing with knights and spectators for the tournament. Only with great difficulty did she find a place to stay.

"I should have come straight here and not spent two days in the Larchental," she thought. "I enjoyed helping Tresson, but if one is to compete at jousting, one must think of nothing else. Now I am already at somewhat of a disadvantage, in having to stay at a place where it will be noisy every night and difficult to get any sleep."

The entire city seemed to be in confusion, due to the preparations for the event. The advantage of a big tournament was that the prizes were larger, and there were more of them. However, the contest itself was much more difficult. There were so many knights that it was simply not possible to study them all in advance and develop a strategy for each one.

In addition, knights came to compete from many different regions, each of which had its own fighting style. That made the tournament more interesting for those who were fighting solely for the honour of it, but for those who had to earn a living from the prize money, it was a serious handicap. Igravaine knew it was quite possible that she might win nothing at all, in which case she would have to make her winnings from Beckern last as long as she could.

For the first two days of jousting, she did not do badly and, thanks to Gryphon, even won a small prize for horsemanship. However, on the third day, her luck failed. There had been a light snowfall, and the ground was very slippery. In the first clash, both horses lost their footing, and she was forced to continue the fight on foot with her sword. Her opponent's sword was longer than her own, and in the fierce combat that followed, she received a heavy blow on her sword arm.

Realising immediately that her arm was broken, she lowered her sword to concede the fight. She managed to get help in setting and binding her arm but knew that she was in a very difficult situation. A knight with a broken sword arm was more than half helpless, and she was in a crowded city, where she knew no one.

Tresson had said, "You know you are welcome to come here..." Surely he would be willing to give her and Gryphon a place to stay until her wound had healed, and then she could repay him by helping with the farm work. The pass would be dangerous if the snow stayed on the ground. However, if she and Gryphon travelled day and night, they might be able to reach the Larchental in three days.

In fact, it was four days later by the time they had crossed the pass, after plodding for hours through driving snow and rain. Fortunately, the pass was free of ice, but by the time they reached the Larchental, Igravaine was feverish and exhausted.

When he saw them coming, Tresson guessed at once that something was seriously wrong and ran to meet them. Igravaine seemed only half conscious. He tried to help her down from the saddle but jarred her arm as he did so, which brought her back to life.

"Broken sword arm," she muttered, using her natural voice for the first time. "Slight fever, and fatigue. You don't mind keeping us until I get better?" Tresson put his arm around her to make sure she didn't fall as they crossed the courtyard.

For two days Igravaine had a high fever and could eat nothing. Tresson was very anxious, but finally her fever grew less. He watched over her constantly, giving her the best food that he had, and gradually she started to recover, and her arm began to heal.

As soon as her fever was gone, Igravaine began asking Tresson what kind of work she could do to repay him and to help make up for the time he had lost in taking care of her. However, he insisted that she must first regain her full strength. "Otherwise, I won't be getting a very good bargain," he said, jokingly.

In reality, he was very worried. He had been shocked to see Igravaine injured and knew that another time, she might lose her life. He made up his mind that under no circumstances was he going to let her leave and go back to jousting. However, he realised it would be impossible to keep her by force, as she was completely fearless and a seasoned fighter. In any case, it could never be considered honourable to force a knight to do something against his or her own will. Thus, he would have to persuade her to stay voluntarily. But how?

To give himself time to think, he took Gryphon from the stables and hid him on another part of the farm. Every day he visited Gryphon to groom and ride him, and he let Gryphon and Beaugard run together, which they both loved. Tresson's idea was that if Gryphon was hidden, he could be sure that Igravaine would not leave unexpectedly.

When Igravaine asked Tresson how long she should work to repay him, he said, "A good six weeks," which she seemed to think perfectly fair.

She loved living in the Larchental because it was so beautiful and became very interested in the cheese-making operation. "Tresson is lucky," she thought. "He can live here all the time, riding Beaugard whenever he likes, with nothing to worry about except how much milk the cows are giving. It seems almost like heaven compared with that chaotic tournament in Drayberg!"

At first, she made no complaint when Tresson told her that Gryphon was at pasture. However, when winter arrived, and deep snow covered the ground, she began to worry that Gryphon was being kept from her because something had happened to him. She asked Tresson if Gryphon was all right and said that she wished to see him at once.

Tresson said, "Upon my honour, Gryphon is completely healthy. He was tired from the journey over the pass but recovered in only a few days. Of course, you may see him at any time, but first I would like you to consider something."

"Speak your mind then," said Igravaine. She could feel that Tresson was anxious about something.

"When you left for Drayberg," he began, "I feared that all would not be well. It grieves me to the heart to think of you going always from joust to joust, barely making a living, and likely, sooner or later, to receive your deathblow. I would do anything to persuade you to remain here with me. The best that I can offer you is that we should marry and become partners in the business, and that you should share in everything with me. Indeed, if you would prefer not to do any fixed work but would rather ride all day with Gryphon through the woods and grassland, of course that would be your free choice. Or even if you wished, from time to time, to attend a joust for pleasure, that to me would still be far better than doing it constantly. I beg you to consider whether you could be happy here!"

"I am greatly honoured by your offer," replied Igravaine. "With your leave, I will take some time to consider it."

No one could help admiring Tresson. Even though he preferred farming to fighting, he was an honourable knight and certainly loved her. However, she was still concerned about Gryphon. She suspected where he might be and decided to look for him.

At her first opportunity, she slipped away unobserved and made her way on skis to the valley where she had helped Tresson build a bridge on her first morning in the Larchental. At the edge of the valley, she saw tracks going down and did not hesitate to follow them.

A whinny greeted her as she reached a sheltered spot. Not far from the place where she and Tresson had sat and eaten lunch was a tiny stable, just large enough to hold two horses and a supply of hay. She unfastened her skis and ran over to the stable entrance. Gryphon looked fresh and healthy, and he and Beaugard looked almost smug, as if to say, "I'm sure you wish you were as well looked after as we are!"

Igravaine threw her arms around Gryphon's neck. "You like it here, don't you?" she asked. "Even better than travelling all the time with me and jousting. If Tresson can take such good care of you, I think I can be happy with him too."

She heard a shout from behind her. "Igravaine! You're not leaving, are you?" Tresson came skiing down the slope.

"No," she laughed. "I just wanted to talk things over with Gryphon. He seems so pleased with his life here, that we've decided we would both like to be farmers and stay here with you."

Tresson was extremely happy and relieved. He and Igravaine lost no time in getting married and lived happily in the Larchental for a very long time.

THE LIZARD WHO SAVED THREE VILLAGES

THIS is a tale about a friend of the Red-Gold Dragon:

Once upon a time, a small green lizard lived among the ruins of a temple high on a hilltop, which overlooked three villages scattered along the seacoast. The roof of the temple had rotted away, but the stone pillars, carved in the shape of human figures, were still standing. The columns, or caryatids, on the east side of the temple had the form of beautiful maidens, while those on the west side resembled handsome young men.

The climate was hot and sunny, and terraced grape vines had been planted over most of the hillside. Each day, after hunting for food among the rocks and shrubs near the temple, the lizard climbed up one of the columns and rested on the hot stone while basking himself in the sun. In the morning, when the sun was in the east, he would choose one of the caryatids on the east side of the temple, and in the afternoon, when the sun was in the west, he preferred one of the pillars resembling a young man on the west side of the temple.

One morning, as he was perched, half asleep, on the arm of a caryatid carved in the form of a maiden with long, flowing hair, he thought he heard female voices. For a moment, he thought that perhaps the caryatids were speaking to one another and that he must be asleep and dreaming. However, then the voices grew louder, and he could begin to understand what they were saying.

"You see," said one voice, "it is as I said. From here we can see clearly down into the winemakers' village below us."

"You are right," agreed a second voice. "All the streets and courtyards are visible."

The lizard crept cautiously up to the shoulder of the caryatid, so that he could peer around the side of the pillar. Standing near the front of the temple, intently studying the village below, were seven maidens who, from their dress, must have come from the village to the east. The lizard soon gathered from what they said that they planned to rob the winemakers' village, which lay directly south of the temple.

"What fools they are to put their wine into bottles at a time when their largest ships are away at sea!" exclaimed one of the maidens. "Now the wine will be easy to steal, and they will not be able to defend themselves.”

“Usually they are not so careless,” answered another maiden. “I heard they are planning a wedding for the head winemaker’s daughter, and they imagine that their voyages of preparation are a secret. Fortunately, our sentinels recognised their ships as they departed.”

From the conversation, the lizard learned that the villagers to the east, who lived mainly by fishing, had a great liking for white wine and planned to steal as much of it as possible. The seven maidens had been sent to the temple as scouts, to plan the best route through the village reach to the cellars where the wine was kept.

“Tomorrow night there will be a full moon and a high tide,” said the maiden who seemed to be the oldest. “We can land at the innermost part of the harbour, close to the village. Then we have only two lanes to go up, to reach the largest wine cellars. Do you see? They are there, by those arches. We will bring tools with us to open the doors."

The youngest maiden was the only one who disagreed. "Their ships are bigger than ours. If we take their wine, we will destroy their trade. They will certainly be angry and will attack our village."

However, the other maidens refused to listen to her. "When will we have such a good opportunity again?" they argued. "The winemakers' village is wealthy. They make both red and white wine. If we take the white wine, the red wine will still be left. We will disguise ourselves, so that even if they see us, they will not be sure who has robbed them. It will not be worth their while to attack us."

After they had memorised the route they would take, the maidens left the temple. Except for the youngest, they were all laughing and joking with one another about how good the wine would taste. As they passed beneath him, the lizard kept perfectly still so as not to attract their attention. Only the youngest maiden glanced up at him for an instant as she went by.

The lizard watched them make their way down a path on the far side of the hill, out of sight of the winemakers' village. An hour later, he saw them arrive at a small, rocky inlet on the seacoast far below, where a boat lay waiting for them. The boat headed to the east, keeping close to the shoreline so as not to be seen. Hoping there would be no more disturbances, the lizard resumed his interrupted nap.

At noon it was very hot as he descended from the pillar to search for his midday meal. He then made his way to the west side of the temple and climbed up a pillar carved in the form of a young man armed with a bow and arrows. The lizard stretched himself out in the sun and closed his eyes.

He was half asleep when he thought he heard the shuffle of footsteps on the stone floor of the temple and then the sound of male voices. At first, he imagined that the pillars were speaking to one another and that he was asleep and dreaming. However, then he realised that, as before, it was not a dream. The voices grew louder, and he began to understand what they were saying.

"What fools they are to leave their village unprotected!" exclaimed a voice. "From here we can see every lane and archway."

The lizard crept silently to the top of the carved bow shaft, where he could get a better view. Near the front of the temple, looking down at the village below, were seven young men. They were dressed for hunting, and from this the lizard guessed that they must have come from the village to the west.

He was astonished to hear the same conversation which had taken place in the morning, repeated almost exactly by a group of young men in the afternoon. However, it soon became apparent that it was the red wine which interested the villagers to the west.

"There will be a high tide soon after dark tomorrow night," said the man who seemed to be the oldest. "If we land at the western end of the harbour, we shall be close to the cellars where the red wine is kept. You see? They are there, beside the bell tower."

As before, it was only the youngest of the group who objected to the plan. "If we rob the winemakers, they will become our enemies. After their big ships return, it is we who will be in danger."

However, the other young men refused to listen. "Why should they begrudge us a few bottles of wine? We will take only the red wine; the white wine will still be left. It will not be worth their while to make trouble for us."

After they had memorised the route they would take, the young men left the temple, joking about how good the wine would taste. As they passed by, only the youngest, who remained silent, happened to glance up and catch sight of the lizard watching them. The young men disappeared down a path on the far side of the hill. Looking toward the sea, the lizard saw a waiting boat lying hidden at the mouth of a stream.

He tried to resume his interrupted nap, but his thoughts made him very uncomfortable. If the winemakers were robbed of both their red and white wine, it seemed certain that serious fighting among the three villages would be the result. The temple itself would be in danger. Traditionally, it belonged to all three villages since it was the only place that could be reached easily from all three. Even though the temple was old and no longer had a roof, no one had dared to remove any of the beautifully carved pillars, for fear of angering the other villagers. However, if fighting broke out, how long would the pillars be left standing? The winemakers might even decide to destroy the temple, since it provided such a good vantage point for spying on their village.

That night the lizard had nightmares about fighting and crashing columns. He woke very early in the morning and in the first light, stared down at the winemakers' village, studying it as carefully as the enemy scouts had done the day before and noting the location of the various cellars and laneways. As he was watching, he saw a young woman with a basket leaving a house near the centre of the village. He recognised her by her green and gold head scarf as the woman who came almost every day to work in the fields below the temple. Having observed the position of her house, he made up his mind what to do.

First, he circled the temple, searching for food. As he passed each of the columns, he glanced up at the carved figures, hoping that his plan would be successful and that he would soon be back at the temple.

After eating as much as he could, he began descending the hill, keeping the sun on his left side. He kept out of sight as much as possible, choosing a route beneath rocky ledges and under the branches of spiny shrubs, since he knew that a lizard was as tasty a delicacy for a hawk or an eagle as a beetle was for a lizard.

The sun grew hotter and hotter. He longed to stop and take a nap, as he usually did in the morning but knew that he must keep moving. Just before noon, when the sun had become so bright that it seemed pale in the sky above him, he reached the first row of grape vines which stretched across the hillside. At the end of the row was a path, descending from one terrace to the next.

He began following the path, keeping watch overhead and pausing every few minutes to listen. At last, there was the sound of someone at work among the grape vines. He crept nearer and heard the voice of a young woman humming to herself. When she raised her head, he could see her green and gold scarf.

She was digging up weeds and putting them into her basket to take down to the village, to feed the goats. While she was looking the other way, the lizard darted toward the large basket that was resting on the ground and climbed carefully up the far side of it, where she could not see him.

Finally, he could take a nap. He closed his eyes. If he could stay hidden on the basket, he would be carried down to the village at the end of the day. Late in the afternoon, he managed to find something to eat. Soon after he had returned to the basket, bells began to toll in the village below, signalling the workers in the fields to return home. The young woman strapped the basket onto her back, picked up her water jug and descended the hill to the village.

The lizard clung tightly to the basket. When she arrived home, the young woman went first to the place where the goats were, to feed them the weeds she had brought back with her. As she set down the basket, the lizard sped away and hid himself under the eaves of the house. The first part of his plan had succeeded. He was now in the village.

He waited until all the lanes were quiet and most of the lights in the village had been put out. Then, finding his way by moonlight, he crept along the lanes to the large cellars where most of the white wine was kept.

There were three cellars close together. The doors of the first two were tightly fastened, and there were no cracks big enough for a lizard to squeeze through. However, the third cellar had a large space beneath the door, and the lizard crept inside.

It was cool and damp, very different from the warm, sunny hilltop where the temple was. The second part of the lizard's plan was to create a disturbance, to alert the winemakers before the robbers could arrive. He had not been able to plan exactly what he would do, since he did not know what he would find in the cellars.

Since it was completely dark inside the cellar, the lizard could explore only by feel and smell. First he came to great, heavy, wooden wine casks and then to crates of empty bottles, resting on the floor. Finally, at the back of the cellar, he found a shelf crowded to the edge with glass wine bottles standing upright. Most of them had been filled with wine and were too heavy for him to move. However, several bottles at one end of the shelf were still empty.

By using all his strength, the lizard was able to move one of the empty bottles, little by little, toward the edge of the shelf. After several minutes of shoving against the slippery glass, he managed to force the bottle far enough forward so that it tottered at the edge and then plunged into a crate of empty bottles below, with a great crash of breaking glass.

He immediately began to work on a second bottle. A neighbour across the street was just looking out, ready to lock his front door for the night, when the second bottle crashed to the floor of the cellar. Startled by the sound, the neighbour quickly crossed the street and listened at the door of the cellar. The lizard had found a bottle that was already part way over the edge of the shelf. Once again, there was the sound of breaking glass. The neighbour went to get help.

Since the family who owned the cellar were already asleep, it was some time before the neighbour could convince them that there were vandals at work. By that time, several households had been awakened. The lizard had begun to work on the seventh bottle when the door of the cellar was flung open, and the light of several lanterns shone into the darkness.

The shards of the broken bottles were plain to see. However, the lizard was so dazzled by the sudden light that he was unable to avoid the glare of the lanterns.

"Look, it is a lizard who is doing it!" someone exclaimed. The lizard swiftly darted out of sight behind the full wine bottles.

In spite of having seen him among the empty bottles, after the first exclamation, the winemakers could not really believe that a lizard had caused the damage. They shone their lanterns into every corner of the cellar, searching for another culprit but could find nothing.

As the winemakers argued about what might have happened, their children, who had taken advantage of the chance of escaping from their beds after dark, were darting up and down the laneways, playing tag and hide-and-seek. Suddenly they all came racing back to the cellar, breathless with excitement.

"Papa, Mama! A boat with no lights and no sails is coming into the harbour. We saw it in the moonlight!"

The lizard sighed with relief. This was what he had hoped would happen. The warning had been given.

Filled with surprise, the winemakers hurried to the harbour. When the robbers from the village to the east saw the approaching lanterns, they knew they had no hope of secretly stealing the wine. Silently, before they could be recognised, they rowed as quickly as possible out to sea. The winemakers arrived at the shore just in time to see the boat disappearing past the eastern headland of the harbour. It was not difficult to guess that this was an enemy ship from the village to the east. Disturbed by the sight of a strange ship in their harbour, several of the winemakers decided to patrol the whole village, searching for hidden enemies.

The lizard wondered whether it would be necessary to carry out the next part of his plan. He crept out of the cellar and along back lanes, past the bell tower, to the stone cellars where the red wine was kept. He could find no way into the first two cellars but managed to enter the third through a gap between two stones.

This time, there were no empty bottles perched on a shelf. He explored the whole cellar and finally discovered a valve on one of the huge casks. The valve was so well-oiled that he was able to turn it, little by little, until wine began to splash out of the cask onto the stone floor of the cellar.

Only a few moments later, the heavy door was flung open, and lantern light flooded the cellar. As before, the lizard was momentarily blinded by the sudden light. He fled to hide behind the casks but not before he had been seen clinging to the valve.

"A lizard has opened the valve!" exclaimed one of the men in astonishment.

However, after the first moment, the winemakers thought surely there must be some other explanation. They turned off the valve and shone their lanterns into every corner of the cellar but could find nothing unusual.

The lizard listened as the winemakers searched other cellars nearby. Then he heard someone say,

"We should go down to the water, to make sure no boats are hidden by the shore."

The lizard followed cautiously to see what would happen. As the winemakers reached the top of a narrow passageway which led down to the water, a shadowy group of figures, without lights, could be seen silently approaching. The moment the strangers caught sight of the gleam of lanterns above them, with one accord they turned and fled.

The winemakers, startled and angry, pursued the fleeing figures. They recognised the hunting dress of the people from the village to the west but were not in time to prevent them from escaping in their boat.

The lizard managed to find his way back to the house where the young woman lived. He entered through a front window which had been left ajar, and the first thing he saw, standing in a patch of moonlight, was the large basket. He crawled into it, hid under a piece of cloth, and fell asleep.

He was so tired that he did not wake up until he was halfway up the hillside again. The basket was being carried on the back of the young woman with the green and gold scarf, who was talking to a man walking beside her.

To his consternation, the lizard heard the man giving a description of the type of lizard that had been seen in the two cellars. "A small green lizard, with bright eyes, an alert look and quick movements."

"That type of lizard does not live in our village," said the young woman. "It is found only near the top of the hill, by the temple."

"Come up to the temple with me," suggested the man. "Perhaps we will learn something."

She agreed, and the lizard found himself being carried all the way to his home. As soon as the young woman set down her basket on the temple steps, he escaped and climbed up his favourite caryatid.

He was safely back at the temple, but had he succeeded in preventing a battle among the three villages? The two people scanned the seacoast and turned their gaze toward first the eastern and then the western village. They spoke in low voices, and the lizard could catch only the phrases, "I will report to the Council," and "We must certainly patrol every night, until our ships return."

After leaving the temple, the young woman resumed work in the field where she had been the day before, and the man returned to the village.

Late in the afternoon, a group of people from the winemakers' village climbed up the steep slope to the temple, carrying wine jars and bowls. The lizard watched in amazement as they carefully placed a bowl of wine at the foot of each of the carved pillars. Bowls of white wine were placed along the east side of the temple, and bowls of red wine along the west side.

Wondering what was going to happen next, instead of concealing himself in a crevice for the night as he usually did, at dusk the lizard returned to his favourite caryatid and stretched himself out along her arm.

He was awakened near midnight by laughing voices and flickering lights approaching the temple. He saw seven maidens advancing by torchlight and recognised them as the scouts from the village to the east.

"Look behind us! We had better wait to see who they are," came the voice of the oldest maiden.

In a few minutes, a second group, also bearing torches, drew near the temple. The lizard recognised the seven young men from the village to the west.

"Why have you come here?" challenged the oldest maiden.

"We heard the news, as you did," answered the oldest of the young men.

"And what did you hear?"

"That last night, the gods of the temple sent one their number, in the form of a lizard, to alert the winemakers, so that they would not lose their wine to robbers. In gratitude, the winemakers have revived their ancient custom of offering a bowl of wine to each of the figures represented on the pillars."

"So," replied the maiden. "But it is the ancient custom of our village to sample the white wine, offered to the caryatids on the east side of the temple."

The young man laughed. "And it is the ancient custom of our village to sample the red wine, offered at the west side of temple. Let us not argue but set to work."

In a few moments, the scouts had moved all the bowls of wine to the centre of the temple. Soon laughter could be heard, interspersed with serious but mostly admiring comments about the quality of the wine. The lizard could not help wondering if, in addition to paying homage to the gods, the winemakers had brought the wine to the temple as a way of pacifying their neighbours and, at the same time, possibly expanding the market for the wine.

He did not notice until it was too late that the youngest maiden had wandered away from her friends and was shining her torch here and there. Before he realised what she was doing, she had caught sight of him on the arm of his favourite caryatid. Since there was no path of escape except to the top of the column, the lizard stayed where he was. Perhaps the maiden meant him no harm.

The youngest of the men had noticed the maiden searching among the pillars and came to join her.

"Are you looking for the lizard?" he whispered as he approached.

Silently, she raised her torch a little, so that the lizard was plainly visible.

"How did you know? I saw him when we came here to plan what to do."

"I saw him too, but then he was on a pillar at the west side of the temple."

"I am sure he is a real lizard. He wanted to save us from making enemies of the winemakers."

The young man looked at her in surprise. "I have the same opinion! Do you know what I heard? The winemakers plan to construct a statue of a lizard in the main square of their village."

The maiden laughed softly. "Will you like that?" she asked the lizard. However, the lizard only blinked his eyes to show that he had heard. Then she and the young man walked slowly toward the steps of the temple and gazed down at the winemakers' village. Everything was still, except for the lights of a patrol.

After the return of their big ships, the winemakers built a large statue of a lizard in their village square. The lizard could see it clearly from the temple. He guessed that as well as commemorating the rescue of the wine, it was intended as a reminder to the other villages of their unsuccessful attempt at a raid, and a warning not to attempt such a deed again.

The young people of the villages to the east and west had enjoyed their midnight gathering so much that they frequently met at the temple after that. The two youngest seemed to have an especially good understanding with one another. They often wandered about together, and the lizard sometimes allowed them to catch sight of him.

"There he is!" the maiden would exclaim. "Think of his courage and intelligence, to have saved our three villages from fighting one another."

"Yes," the young man would reply, "and now he is a hero, with a statue built to him in the main square!"

After the statue was completed, the winemakers took care never to leave their village unguarded, and peace reigned in the region for many years.

9 781777 383459